After YOU

RISHITA PAUL

After YOU

RISHITA PAUL

KALAMOS LITERARY SERVICES LLP

Kalamos Literary Services LLP
Email: info@kalamos.co.in | editorial@kalamos.co.in
First Published in 2021
by
Kalamos Literary Services

ISBN- 978-93-90909-82-7

Rishita Paul
After You

Typeset in Kalamos Literary Services LLP

Cover designed by Brand Inspire OPC Pvt. Ltd.
Print and bound in India.

To,
All my readers out there.

1

31st March, 3010
Somewhere on Earth….

I stood with a blank face hoping for the drama to get over. I was too dumb to fight. My silence and stillness made them even more angry. I was so tired and exhausted that I hardly had any power to even stand. They had beaten me the hell out. But still I managed to stand making eye contact with them which boiled their anger. It was when they punched me right in my left eye that I fell down.

I opened my eyes only to realize that I have blacked out. I managed to sit up straight and then slowly stood up. They were gone. The bullies were gone. How heartless are they!

I had a crush on my classmate. I didn't even do anything. I just used to admire her throughout the entire day, and may be that was my mistake and she informed this 'mischievous' act of mine to her brothers and rest was history.

Today was the last day of our exam. I wished to spend it peacefully, but no, when there's an existence of bullies, forget about peace, you can't even breath properly. I grabbed my school tablet and scoot-walker, *(a scoot-walker is an advanced vehicle used by the people in 3010)* got on it and made my way out of my classroom and reached the corridor. I realized that my knees were badly bleeding, and I was sweating heavily even in the presence of an AC. Since the past few decades, the sun has grown really hot and it literally sucks. I tapped on the 'walk fast' button and hurriedly made my way towards the washroom. The sensor door opened, and I got in. I extended my hands underneath the tap and cold water started pouring down. I splashed my face with some cold water and looked at my reflection on the mirror and realized that my left eye has got swollen and turned blue. I touched it and shrieked in pain.

'One day I'll surely teach those bullies a lesson' I murmured under my breath.

After few minutes I found myself on the road, on my way towards home. My knees were bleeding so much that I could barely manage to even stand on my walker. I noticed my walker was running out of charge. 10%. I panicked. After moving some more distance, I noticed a girl, she was seated under a tree and looked like as if she's engrossed in some deep thinking. And then suddenly I felt a jerk and stumbled with my walker and fell down. I realized the charge has gone out. The girl hurriedly came towards me and helped me to stand.

'Are you okay?' she said.

'Yeah, I am. Thanks' I said.

'Oh my god! Your knee is bleeding!' she exclaimed.

'Yeah…' I said sheepishly.

'How did that happen?' she asked.

'Um… some fights you know…' I managed to say.

'Let me help you.' She said and took out her first aid kit.

Meanwhile I was getting first aid, I decided to talk to her. She looked really different and strange. Yet she was so beautiful. I couldn't take my eyes off her. Her glass-skin was so attractive and unique.

'Am Aiden' I said trying to initiate a conversation.

'Am Ariel.' She said and smiled.

'Do you live here?' I asked and she fumbled with the right words and said, 'Um, no actually I don't live here, I've come here for some work…'

'Oh, okay' I said.

Once my first aid was done, I got up to leave but realized my walker was out of charge. Then Ariel insisted me on taking her walker. I didn't know why an unknown strange girl was offering me to take her walker, but having no other choice, I agreed.

'I'll return it tomorrow.' I said.

'Sure, no problem!' she smiled.

'But how you'll reach your home?' I asked.

'Oh, don't worry about that! I'll manage.' She said.

I didn't understand anything but yet nodded in agreement and left.

Once I was home, I found myself still thinking about her. For a moment I forgot I had a crush for which I got beaten up today.

I put my walker into charge and changed into comfy clothes.

I was hungry so I ordered Roboco, my maid robot to make some dish for me. And within no time my dish was right on the table. I sat down and began eating when my eyes stopped on Ariel's walker which lay just beside the sofa.

'Looks-like-you-bought-a-new-walker-Mr.-Aiden' Roboco said.

'I met a girl today, she lent me hers, my walker was dead today on my way.' I said.

'Great! -Mr.- Aiden' Roboco said and got back to her work.

I wondered what Ariel was doing right now.

2

The next day afternoon, I went to the same place on my scoot-walker along with hers but couldn't find her. And after sometime, she suddenly emerged from somewhere and appeared infront of me.

'Hi!' Ariel said.

'Hey, here's your walker.' I said returning her the walker.

'Thanks!'

'So, where are you from?' I asked her.

'Actually, I have come here for some research and the place where I live is quite far away' she said.

I didn't know what to respond. So, instead I told her if she's up for having some ice-cream and she agreed.

Together we made our way towards the ice-cream parlor on our respective Scoot-walker.

'What's your age?' she asked me.

'Well, am 17, you?'

'Oh! Am 15.' She said and I was surprised. I mean she doesn't look like 15. She looked so mature and adult. I also noticed her eyes were sky-blue and lips- perfect pink, pinker than the pink color actually.

The more time I spent with her, the more I was falling for her! I couldn't dare to ask if she already has someone in her life.

As we were riding on our scoot-walker side by side, I couldn't help but steal glances from her, she was too occupied by the surroundings to notice, and finally she turned towards me leaving me baffled. I immediately turned away and blushed.

'Do you like this place?' I said.

She was quite for a few seconds and then said, 'Yeah! I do.' She said and smiled sheepishly.

'Hey, why don't you come over to my place!' I said and instantly regretted for saying it.

'Um, no thanks some other day.' She said.

We reached the ice-cream parlor, there were two robots making ice-creams for customers.

'Welcome-sir-which-flavor-do-you-wanna-have.' The female robot said.

'Um, I would have one butterscotch and…' I turned around to ask Aerial which flavor she wants, but she was disappeared.

I looked around but couldn't trace her. After few seconds I spotted her at some distance. I approached her.

'Here' I said handing the ice-cream to Aerial.

'Thanks' she said.

The sunset looked really amazing, with Aerial beside me, it was more beautiful. She looked more ravishing. I still couldn't figure out why she was so flawless and beautiful as compared to the other people in this city. I don't know why I was falling for her in the first place when I knew barely about her. I don't even know where she lives.

'So' I began, 'For how long you're here?'

She looked at me, thought for a second and then said, 'I don't know, my team will connect with me as soon as they…' she paused and then continued, 'I mean as soon as my research is over.'

I just wanted to confess her the very moment and let her know that how much I have started caring for her and adoring her. It was surprising how I forgot all my worries and tensions whenever I was with her.

Just then my phone rang, it was Roboco.

'Your-dinner-is-ready-Aidan-see-you-soon.' She said.

'I think we must go now, it's already late.' Aerial said and I nodded and we both stood up.

She signaled me to head forward.

'After you' I said and she took the lead and we both rode off with our walkers.

'Are we meeting tomorrow?' I said, my heart already beating fast.

'Probably' she said.

I reached home and saw Roboco waiting for me. After I was done with my dinner, I decided I would confess Aerial about my feelings and let her know everything what I feel. I have fallen in love with her. I am not sure if she likes me but still, I'll go for it.

It was when I went to bed and decided to play some games on my phone that I realized I didn't have Aerial's phone number. I wish I had, so I could call and talk to her. I casually opened the contact section of my phone and started scrolling through the list when I accidently tapped on my own number and it started ringing, before I could hang up, someone picked up my call. I was stunned.

'Hello?' someone said. It was a male voice.

I didn't know what to respond.

'Hello?' I said panicky.

'Hey! Earth resident! Thank you for calling us!' he said.

Before I could say anything he already started blabbering.

'We have been trying to get in touch with you since very long, now that you have connected with us, let me tell you that we belong to a very far place from Earth. A girl has been sent to Earth but unfortunately, we lost connection with her and our spaceship is under repair. Due to which we are unable to get her back. So, if you come across with her by anyhow, please let us know, it's really very urgent.' He said.

I was speechless, I couldn't understand what the hell was happening with me, for a moment I thought it was a dream but it was real! A call from another planet!!!!!!!! I wanted to scream.

'Hello? Are you there Mr.?' he said.

'Yeah, tell me? Any description about her?' I said and gulped.

And then what he said has freaked me the hell out. The description which he gave almost matched with Aerial. I couldn't breathe. I didn't tell them that I had already came across her but also promised to inform them if I come across. I don't know why did I do that. I was told not to disclose this thing to anyone. I was left speechless. It was hard for me to digest that the person with whom I happen to fall in love was someone who was out of my planet. Is she an alien? I couldn't sleep. I panicked. Why is she here? What does she want? And why did they call me specifically? I wish I didn't know. I felt guilty. Now I was able to connect the dots, why was she reluctant in letting me know where she lived and why she came here. Here I was planning to propose to her and now? What am I gonna do now?

3

I didn't want to show my face to Aerial. I couldn't even understand how I was feeling. My heart was broken. So many dreams I have visualized with Aerial, but everything was crushed into pieces. I have never ever fallen in love before. This love felt so unreal and special yet I couldn't do anything about it.

'You look pale, everything okay Aidan?' Aerial said.

She never fails to read my face.

'Yeah, okay. Didn't have enough sleep.' I said.

'Oh! No problem. It happens.' She said.

'Don't you miss your home?' I asked.

'Um, why?'

'It's because, I don't even know where you are from and you don't even tell me why you came here.' I said, 'I mean in this city.' I didn't want to let her know that I knew she came from another planet. Although I didn't know specifically from which planet she came from.

'Yes, sometimes I do.' She smiled and looked away.

Never have I ever seen such a gentle and kind girl in my entire life. All the girls I have ever met till today were either rude, arrogant or hated me, she was the first girl-friend of mine who didn't seem to have got pissed off me.

'Don't you find me infuriating?' I asked.

'What? No, why?' she laughed.

'No, I mean girls of my class find me annoying and terrible. So, I thought—'

'So? Doesn't mean I'll find you too. Different people have different opinions.' She said.

'So, what opinion do you have about me?'

'Um. Let me think' she said, 'You are a mature, understanding and a kind hearted person.' It melted my heart. Everyone I knew has always assumed me as a childish and an immature person. Aerial was the first person who has considered me a mature one and it drives me crazy. Am already on cloud nine.

'That's so sweet of you.' I said and blushed.

We kept talking and laughing and smiling all the way through. Whenever I was with her, I loved myself even more. By loving her, I got to know about the deep emotions of love. By loving her, I got to know how powerful love can be. I found myself falling in love with her even more than I could ever think of. I didn't want to lose her. Ever.

4

We kept meeting for days and days and the more I was with her, the more I loved her. And the more I loved her, the more I had fears of losing her. No matter how much time I spend with her, this guilt of not letting her know about the call from her planet was eating me up. It was when we were seated beside the riverside and watching the stars and moon and she told me something which made me feel guilty even more.

'The sky looks so clear today, isn't it?' Aerial said and I nodded.

I looked at her and she looked immensely beautiful under the moonlight. I wanted to pull her cheeks and look deep into her eyes and never ever return from there. It felt so magical to be with her. I have never ever felt this way for any girl. I don't know if it was due to because she didn't belong to our planet or whatsoever but I truly wanted to be with her. I noticed her eyes were twinkling more than the previous time.

After few minutes of silence, I noticed that she was sobbing silently. I asked her what was wrong but she denied, and after asking several times more, she said she misses her home. Most importantly she misses her sister. She has no one except her. I didn't know what to say. I knew she wasn't talking about 'Earth'. And finally, she said, 'I want to confess something Aidan.'

'At first, I was afraid of you when you began asking me about my whereabouts, although I didn't show you but I thought you were a spy and was told to gather information about a mysterious girl. Which was me. A few of the residents of this locality has already come to know that a girl has been sent to Earth for some secret mission, they think am some strange creature or an alien, although they haven't seen me yet, they have just discovered some proof, am not here for any secret mission, I was just sent here for an important research which was necessary for our planet. I was meant to stay here for a very short time, but my computerized bracelet stopped working and I lost touch with my planet, am stuck here for a month, I don't know how am I gonna return to my home. But then when you started meeting me daily, I began trusting you that you weren't any spy, so you are the only one who knows this, please don't tell this to anybody. Aidan.'

I got goosebumps. I couldn't believe this is the same girl I have fallen in love with.

I struggled to find the right words to speak.

'We have a secret group in our planet where each one of them are sent to different planets for various types of research, once in every three years and it was my turn to come to Earth. Although our government isn't aware of it, they don't allow these things, so we had to do this secretly.'

'So, you mean you came here illegally?' I said astounded.

'Kind of.' She said, 'But, it isn't that scary as much as it sounds.'

'Please help me Aidan, I want to go back to my home' she said, tears in her eyes.

I felt guilty. I didn't know what to do and what to say her as well.

I went back to my home that night without telling her anything. I couldn't tell her; I was afraid to lose her. How could I just tell her that? If I tell her that yes, her planet has contacted me and now she can happily go back to her home, what about me? What about my love? What if I lose her? Who is going to bear that pain? Me off course! Who is going to handle those? Me off course!

Various thoughts kept hovering over my mind and prevented me from falling asleep. I have never ever felt so much guilty in my entire life.

I grabbed my phone and noticed there were various missed calls from my own number. I tapped on it and called.

'Hello! Earth Resident! Did you able to get any information about Aerial?' he said.

With a heavy heart I said, 'Yes.'

5

The next day I went straight to Aerial, I didn't even have my breakfast, Roboco was shouting and scolding me like anything. I knew I wouldn't be able to digest any sorts of food until and unless I confess to Aerial. No, not about my love for her.

'I want to confess something.' I said. Aerial was fidgeting with her bracelet.

'Hey! Too early? Yeah say, what is it?' she said without looking up.

I went and sat beside her. I blabbered everything which was inside me since the day I received the call. I told her everything, starting from the call to feeling guilty of hiding this, everything.

'I know you must be angry upon me, I am so sorry, Aerial. Please don't break friendship with me, I was scared, I didn't know what to do, I couldn't figure out anything. Please forgive me. I have no friends here except you.'

Aerial smiled and then looked at me.

'Aww Aidan, you're so innocent! It's okay! Why the hell would I blame you? It's obvious to behave this way after discovering something unusual.' She said.

'So, you aren't mad at me?'

'Relax! No, am not'

I felt miserable because I didn't let her know the actual reason of keeping it from her. I couldn't tell her this, atleast after knowing that she belongs to another planet. I can't.

She told me she wanted to talk with her team I handed my phone to her and made her call on my own number. After few rings they picked up. I could see the elite happiness on her face after she connected with her team. It was visible on her face how much she missed her home.

'What did they say?' I asked.

She took a deep breath and said, 'Well, our spaceship is still under repair, it may take a few days more, all thanks to you Aidan, without you it wouldn't have been possible! Thank you so much Aidan!'

I don't know why she was thanking a guy who only hid things from her.

'I have one question, how come is it possible to call on my own number? I mean at first, I didn't realize, I was just casually scrolling through my contacts list when accidentally I called on my own number and someone picked up... I mean how—'

'Relax! Let me tell you, actually when I was in my planet, I learned somewhere that it's actually possible to track any random person's phone number on Earth and connect with them, but that was an exceptional case, most of the times it doesn't work, so when they tracked someone else's phone number, which was you, they called you and instead of their number, your own number was visible on that, you can't view theirs' she said and I was taken aback with that weird information.

'You know Aidan, I am always afraid that if somebody sees me especially those robots here, they'll easily recognize that am from another planet and they'll seize me. That day in ice-cream parlor, I disappeared because I knew those robots will easily track down the location am from and it'll be huge chaos. I can't stay here. Although my research is over.'

I understood how difficult it was for her to stay here, I cursed myself for not letting her know about the call earlier itself.

'Anyway, thank you, now am relieved that I'll soon go back to home. I was scared, when all of a sudden my computerized bracelet stopped working, little did I know their spaceship were also damaged.' She said.

I didn't know whether I was happy that she would finally go back to her home or I was sad because I'll lose her forever.

It was hard to face these strange and different emotions. I have never undergone these types of strange emotions ever in my life.

6

I didn't go to meet her today. What's the point of doing all these things when all she could do was leave me forever? I would have managed had she been an Earth resident, atleast I would have the chance to see her every day. What will I do when she'll leave? These days were atleast a better one than those regular boring days, I didn't know if my life would make any sense to me anymore.

It was almost midnight when I received a call. It was them.

'Hello?' I said.

'Hello! Earth resident! Please inform Aerial that our spaceship is almost repaired and we'll come to take her back within two days.' he said.

My heart died a million little deaths. A death where only my physical body was alive, not my soul.

I cried my heart out that night. Tears kept streaming down my cheeks. I could feel my heart break. I was equally happy for experiencing a divine love that I have never felt in my life and sad for learning that the love I experienced was never meant to last forever. How would I live? It seems strange to have fallen in love with someone whom I barely know, but does only that count? Maybe I don't know her properly but what about the emotions I felt after solely knowing her soul? Sometimes when I looked at her, I felt like I am made for her, I am made just to love her.

These things didn't make sense to me anymore. And why would they? She's leaving after all. That too forever.

I delivered the news to Aerial. She was happy after hearing that her team will come to take her very soon. I only have today. And tomorrow, she'll be gone…forever. I have no idea what will I do after her. After she'll be gone.

At times I felt like running away and never show my face and at times I felt like hugging her and never let her go. I wanted to live my today like tomorrow doesn't exists. I wish it could be possible. I wish I could stop the time or go back to the moment I met her for the first time. I wonder had I been not beaten that day; would I meet Aerial? Had my scoot-walker not run out of charge, would things be different today? I have no answer to these questions yet. I still wonder does Aerial have feelings for me? That doesn't make any sense. Does it?

We spent the entire day together. From watching the sunset to silently gazing the stars, I didn't even realize when time passed. I only had today with her. That too has passed. I can only wait for tomorrow.

7

Sometimes, the day which you least expect to come, always ends up coming fast. Her team called me and informed they'll be here at midnight according to our time zone. It was painful for me to tolerate all these. The days spent with Aerial were a magical one. I wonder how the rest of my life would be like after Aerial was gone.

'Wow, I can't believe am finally going back to my home!' Aerial said, 'Aren't you happy, Aidan?'

'Yeah, am happy for you.' I said. It's not that I was not happy, I was happy, for her. In fact, her returning to her planet was way more important than my love for her at this point.

I could have kept this thing from her, but that would have added only miseries to both us, eventually, her team would come to pick her someday off course. She had to go some day or the other. May be falling in love with her was destined, maybe that's why she got stuck here, so that universe could make me fall in love with her and later make me tolerate pain when she leaves. I wonder had she not stuck here, how things would have been today?

'I don't know what to say Aidan, but I just want to thank you, you were there with me all these days when everybody suspected me, you could have informed and disclosed this to everybody, but you didn't, thank you for that.'

'Oh, it's just nothing, we are good friends right, so don't thank me.'

'Yes, we are, I'll miss you Aidan.' She said and it melted my heart, I wanted to cry but somehow held back.

'Yeah.' I nodded. I prevented myself to show any emotions and feelings to her. I didn't want our last meeting to be a tragedy.

'What? You won't miss me?' she said,

'No, I didn't mean that, I mean I would, yes, I would…" I said and looked away.

'Let's wait for my team' she said.

The night sky was aglow with bright city lights. The pale crescent moon shone like a silvery claw in the night sky. We looked up at the blanket of stars that stretched to infinity.

'Life's so uncertain, isn't it?' I said looking at her who was busy gazing at the stars.

'Yeah, just few days ago, we were complete strangers and look at us now, you helped keep my little secret by not telling anybody!' she said and I grinned.

Indeed. How some people become the most important ones in your life when you least expect them to be. Did I know I would meet such an out of the world girl and fall for her? Off course not, but when am in this situation, I feel it'll too pass. Why not enjoy this moment rather than worrying for what's yet to come? For now, she's with me, I cannot waste this time by worrying for the moment when she'll leave, which is yet to come. I wish I could change certain things. Somethings aren't in our hands and falling in love is one of them.

'Will we ever meet again?' I asked controlling my emotions even when I knew the answer.

She was quiet for some time and then finally spoke.

'I wish I had the answer.' She said and a tear drop crawled down my left cheek, I quickly wiped it away.

Please don't go. I love You. I can't live without you. Please stay. I don't know how I'll survive. I couldn't say, not atleast after knowing this is our last moment. After all, few words are always left unsaid…. Isn't it?

There was a sudden weather change. I knew what it was. The grasses that surrounded us were blowing in the east direction. A cold breeze was followed. We both looked up and noticed there was a tiny ray of light that gradually took shape into a huge object.

This is it. This is the moment. Live it. I said to myself.

'My time has come.' Aerial said and we looked at each other and our eyes met. The moment my eyes were on hers, it felt like an eternity. Until she came close and kissed my cheek.

'I'll miss you Aidan!' she said and I looked at the object which looked like a UFO and it landed smoothly on the ground just behind her. Slowly, the door opened and the stairs slid and hit the ground.

I could see her going far away from me, this time I couldn't control my tears, I was crying. I was broken. I wanted to go with her. She headed towards the UFO and after stepping on one of the stairs, for the last time, she turned around and looked at a helpless Aidan, who was crying like a baby. She waved her right hand towards me, I waved back. I couldn't believe this. It felt like a dream that someone would wake me up from this sooner or later. Soon, the stairs rolled up inside and the door got closed and I could no longer see her. Within a flash, the UFO was vanished. Still. Silence. No movement. I don't know for how long I was in that position. I looked around. No Aerial. No UFO. No nothing. It was just me.

It took me two minutes to reach the place where I met Aerial for the first time. I sat there on the bench, perhaps convincing myself that whatever has happened was real for sure. I casually slid my right hand into my pocket when I felt something was there in it. I took it out to realize that it was Aerial's computerized bracelet. I had no idea how it went there. I tapped somewhere on it to realize that it was working. The screen lit up and showed *'Voice message from Aerial'*

I tapped on it.

Somethings aren't in our hands and falling for you was one of them. I didn't realize it until one day you didn't come to meet me. I realized how important you have become for me. I didn't know if it's right or not. I knew you have already fell for me the moment you confessed that you hid about the fact that my team tried to connect with you. In fact, I fell for you the moment I saw you for the very first time, but realized it only when I felt your absence, that's when I felt how you'd feel when I'll be gone. You could have kept it from me and lie to me, but you didn't, perhaps making me return to my actual place seemed more important to you than your love. What it is if it's not love? I may not have confessed this to you, Aidan, but let me tell you one thing, you were the best thing that has ever happened to me, and am not sure if something like this will ever happen to me anymore. These days with you weren't less than a magical. I don't know how my life would be from now. Maybe we won't ever meet, but we both will remember us. You were the best thing, Aidan.

I cried more than ever. I died a thousand little deaths and also took birth at the same time, after learning how she felt for me.

How can someone be so kind? May be this is why she kissed me before leaving me, forever.

8

Next day…

"The mysterious girl that the whole world was talking about has left no trace, it looks like she has returned where she came from, after some people noticed a huge mark which looked like a UFO might have landed on the grasses near the lake at…"

I switched off the television.

'Why-did-you-do-that' Roboco said.

'It's of no use now.' I said.

I went to the terrace and looked at the sky. It was bright and clear. I wondered.

'Stopping her from leaving wasn't in my hands just like how falling for her wasn't. I'll remember us, Aerial and Aidan.'

THE END